THE

THERAPIST

—·—

FRANK T BIRD

THE PEEPING TOM

It's three-twenty in the arvo, and I'm raging for the day to end.

I'm cracking out the Macallan before four, breaking my one last sacred rule. But these crazies, well, they get to you.

I know I shouldn't call them that. If my Master's degree wasn't fake, I probably wouldn't. I might even call them patients. But I've been too long in this savage country, and I'm telling you that you can't hang around with these nut jobs for long without some risk of character amalgamation.

John is a sex addict — neigh, a sex maniac. Even that's inaccurate. To be one of those, you have to have sex. An addict drying out is still an addict, but how can you dry out from a drug you never take? He isn't dangerous unless you count the risk of him ejaculating in the bread aisle at the supermarket because some double dee single mother is bending over to look at the latest high energy-low carb, half-seeded loaf with chia seeds. He is a man who can barely speak to another human, let alone explore the profound intimacy of hurting someone.

His trousers are custard-cream like those teeth-rotting biscuits from 1987. His Nikes are the type you always see on American couples in their drainpipe jeans with their fanny packs.

"Good morning John. How have you been?" I say, desperately forcing a smile like a constipated man forces a shit.

"Yeah, pretty good. Shall I lie down?" he says.

I nod reluctantly. God, I hope he has showered. I don't want his cum dandruff on my couch.

John closes his eyes like he is about to masturbate. I see everything he does as some depraved act. And that's my problem, not his, but I still despise him for it. And now, since his eyes are closed, I take the opportunity to throw back some whiskey.

"To be honest, I've spent a lot of time at home, Doc," John says. "I tried looking for work on Monday for about twenty-five minutes but couldn't find anything except these two factory jobs, and they both wanted to see CVs, so screw it."

"What do you mean by *screw it*, John?" I've begun my professional interruption early today. I should let him talk so I can get him out of here *pronto,* but my negative emotions are sticking voodoo pins into my frontal cortex.

"I mean, *screw* it, Doc. I don't have a CV, and I don't have the time or energy to make one."

I get it. Masturbation takes a lot of time and energy. Everyone knows that.

"I'm not sure how you could get a job without a CV, John," I tell him. "You might have to make one."

"Nah, I don't think so, Doc. I'm not even sure I *want* a job."

He calls me Doc like it's an eighties movie with Michael J Fox. I'm not a doctor, and I don't advertise myself as such. But I don't correct him because sometimes a strong authority figure helps the process — *sometimes*. Does a part of me enjoy it when a patient calls me 'Doctor'? Maybe, *subconsciously*.

My colleagues jokingly offer to pay for my PhD like I am some brown-toothed tramp on a street corner with turd-crusted trousers and a sign that says *homeless and undereducated*. I get it. I'm a source of entertainment. And, I'll put up with the jokes and offers because it keeps the heat off. But, if I was their academic equal, I know they'd dig into my past, and I can't let that happen.

So no, technically, I'm not a state-qualified therapist. And this whole thing probably does *technically* make me a fraud if you believe in the rights of established corporate-driven frameworks to exercise absolute authority regardless of the continuous proof of their inherent corruption and failure. I don't believe in the system. It was set up by colonialists, and it does nothing more than serve the needs of corporations. Besides, it makes me a better psychologist. I am a clear thinker and a rebel. I'm the James Dean of therapy — or possibly, the Charlie Manson. Time will tell. For now, I do my research, and I use *my* methods. My clients seem to appreciate it.

"John, it's fairly obvious you don't *want* a job, but it is something we should work towards. Should something come up, you mustn't masturbate at work, though. It's not tolerated by workplaces these days. It's not only a firing offence anymore. It's a criminal act."

"Oh, I don't masturbate in the workplace Doc. It's a rule I have."

I can't imagine that's true.

"Is that right, John? What was the last job you had?"

"I worked at McDonald's for a while."

"And did you masturbate at McDonald's, John?"

"I did."

"Okay, so that's not much of a rule, is it?"

"Well, I only did it in the toilet or my car on my lunch break. I never actually did it in the kitchen, which was technically my workplace."

Sometimes the path to becoming a serial killer seems short. Sometimes the anger burns in your perineum like you are squatting over a toaster. From that space, it's just a matter of picking up a paperweight and thumping someone's head in. It's good that we don't use paper anymore, so there are no paperweights. Still, anything could do it — maybe even this half-empty bottle of scotch. But that would be a waste of good scotch.

"So John, what you are saying is that you can masturbate *at* work but not *in* the workplace?"

"Yeah, I guess so."

He pulls his pants out of his intergluteal cleft, sniffs his fingers and wipes snot on his sleeve in a routine that has been refined over decades. These things might be considered socially unacceptable, but in John's case, if he isn't ejaculating on your rug, it's all good.

"Have you been visiting your job provider John?"

"No, I've been too tired."

You never ask a masturbation addict why they are so tired. I learned that at my non-existent college.

"Why are you so tired, John? Have you been staying up all night again?"

Damn those voodoo pins in the cortex.

Anyone who ejaculates constantly will feel exhausted. It's why men pass out instantly after sex or Christmas dinner, or Thanksgiving (for you damn Americans). Turkey contains tryptophan, an amino acid used in the production of melatonin, so it puts you to sleep. I had a client once who tried to use turkey as a date rape drug. He said it didn't work because turkey isn't water soluble, and it made the drink smell like turkey.

I'm not even joking. Welcome to the *savage* country.

Still, turkey has *nothing* on sperm.

"I haven't slept in two days," John says. "Wednesday night was raining, but I still went out obsessing over windows. I can't seem to shake it. Maybe they can cut off my dong like they do with dogs, Doc?"

He says *dong* like he is some salesman from the fifties, and I wonder if I can offer to cut off his dong for him and sell it as a delicacy on the black market.

"I'm not sure that's the best idea, John," I say. "They generally cut off a dog's testicles, not his penis, and neutered dogs still *hump* people's legs. You're better off cultivating gratitude for speedy ejaculation, which is like a fire extinguisher for your desire."

I randomly think about my grandfather and how he referred to masturbation as *shanking*. He was an ex-Navy guy who told filthy jokes, saying things like — *and the guy was shanking* — while doing the actions with his wrist. I loved my grandfather as a kid, but if I met him today, I'd probably hate him. He was a racist and a chauvinist like many of his generation. Occasionally when I drink too much, my grandfather's ghost appears doing the shanking action and laughing.

"A quick *shank* can save you from executing a *lot* of bad ideas," I tell John, who looks concerned at my new vocabulary. "*Shanking* is not the issue here, John. But hiding in people's gardens and spying through windows is."

"Yeah, and it's getting bad, Doc," he says. "I went to my aunties' place on the weekend to help move some furniture. When I left, I saw her bedroom light was on, so I hid in this soaking wet bush in the garden and watched her through the window. She took off her shirt, and her bra was massive. You could probably get two full-size basketballs into it with at least another few inches of space all around, and I don't mean those mini office basketballs. I mean real professional basketballs."

John holds out his arms to show me the size like a bragging tit fisherman.

"I started to pull myself, but it was so cold that I was shaking, and I could barely find my shrunken dong. It was a ridiculous situation, but I was there for forty minutes or something."

"And did you get what you were looking for, John?" I ask.

"No, I did not. The breasts stayed covered. That was the worst thing. I wouldn't have been there for that long if the bra *had* come off, but she was just changing her shirt. She watched TV and ate Doritos in bed for a long time — a *stupidly* long time — and I got excited every time she stood up to do something. Eventually, she closed the curtains, and I was left standing there like a wet loser."

The poor bastard is trapped in a classic shank circle. I've tried to convince John to climax quicker, not because it's good for him since it deepens the habitual pattern at the heart of this whole thing, but because it might save him from such extended sexual encounters as this. Also, it would give him *more time* for other things. The drug is by no means the cure and *does* lead to dependence, but in John's case, *the chase* is the addictive aspect. The result John is looking for — such as the exposure of his aunt's basketballs — may not even happen, so extreme time wastage is *always* possible. If he can learn to climax quicker, he can use the extra time to do an online degree, learn the flute, or do yoga — something more productive and energising.

John is horny and lonely — end of story. Unless we can find him a wife who is too observant to let him slip out and hide in some unsuspecting widow's soaking bush, it will probably be a matter of *managing the symptoms*.

"As we have discussed, John, you need to nurture the feeling that masturbation is good and that *climax* is also good. Remember the exercise where you ask yourself if you will regret the action?"

"Yes, I remember Doc."

"Well, did you do it at your aunt's place?"

"No, I forgot about it. I forget about everything when I'm in the zone."

There's no point trying to convince him he is wrong. It's like walking into a bar and lecturing alcoholics about the pros and cons of drinking. These people are addicts. They *know* their actions are morally and spiritually wrong, but they do them anyway.

"So, how many times have your outings been successful, John?" I ask.

He sits up a bit and stares out of the window at some imaginary Excel spreadsheet.

"Well, I can remember *two* missions that stand out," he says.

"Okay, and how many — *missions* — have you been on?"

"It's been bad for about a year. I'd say at least a hundred missions."

"Thanks, John. So, a hundred missions with two hits, that's a two-per-cent hit rate. What do you think would be your average time spent per mission?"

It's getting to me. I know this because I'm subconsciously drawing breasts in my notepad.

John sits up and taps his fingers like he is calculating string theory.

"Look, it's pretty variable, but I'd say I spend between twenty and forty minutes on a mission — sometimes over an hour, depending on the weather and the degree of action."

I do some swift calculations.

"So if your average mission is thirty minutes and you have done a hundred missions, that's fifty hours of peeping with a return of two per cent, which is one hour. My question for you, John, is, do you believe it is worth spending fifty hours for one hour of pleasure?"

"I would say *yes*, it's worth it, Doc. A prospector sieves through thousands of pans of rubble to find tiny bits of gold. A trader will go through *many* losing trades before finding a win. This is a low-win, high-reward game Doc. I should have become a trader because I am disciplined. It's true that I took up masturbation instead, but if masturbation was a sport, I would have a gold medal."

I don't doubt what he says. I want to shake his hand *and* slap him in the face. John has the look of a man who is trying to justify his loss of sperm, and I am rooting for him. It must be the whisky.

I smile *internally*. A man who spies on people for sexual kicks is proud of his legacy. It's like *psychological art*. He is Vincent Van Cock.

I hope, for John's sake, shanking *does* become a sport. He deserves it for his dedication. Also, it might keep him away from the midnight windows.

One of my clients is an entrepreneur. She says that a true entrepreneur takes a problem and sells the solution or something like that. Maybe the cure for John's addiction is an app that picks up your location as being in someone's garden and triggers an alarm — or, even better, a loud voice — that alerts the resident to your presence.

Attention, resident, there is a wanker on your property.

I realise that I missed most of what John said, and now he has gone quiet. I hope he didn't ask me a question. As a therapist, it's poor form to ask people — particularly those with abandonment issues — to repeat themselves. It can be damaging to the relationship.

Part of me still wants to beat him with the non-existent paperweight, and part of me wants to humiliate him. But, occasionally, part of me called *the therapist* lights up and breaks through like the sun oozing through the gap in the grey mind clouds. And I feel sorry for him, so I stay quiet and hope for the best.

"Tell me something about your Father," I finally say. It's a classic line to get things back on track because people associate it with Freud. The line has practically become a form of inducing trance that uses a familiar object rather than the unfamiliar object in methods like the traditional pattern break. I despise Freud and don't know a lot about him except what I've learned through improvised conversations with my colleagues where we sit with whiskey and cigars nattering about the ideas of dead people. I know the line works on John because he closes his eyes.

I open my drawer, fill a glass with whiskey and take a large swig.

"My dad was quite short," John says. "Shorter than my mum, which I used to find bizarre as he would be on his tiptoes every time they kissed — which was a lot."

"Why did you find that bizarre, John?"

"I'm not sure. I was taught that the man is the *manly* one in a relationship, but he was more like the woman. My mum was more like the man."

"So your mother was quite manly?"

"No, she wasn't at all. She also had big breasts — not as big as my aunties', but they were still full. She always wore dresses and high heels so — "

"And was your dad womanly?"

"No, he was just short. I used to think that my mum was tall and my dad was normal-sized. As I got older, I realised my mum was normal-sized, and my dad was *short* — *n*ot super short like a dwarf, more like an elf or something."

Listening to clients speak about childhood can trigger a therapist's own childhood memories. In this case, I'm thinking about my first ejaculation. It happened on a roller coaster when I was twelve. And, since it was my first roller coaster, I linked the two, concluding that it was *supposed* to happen. There was nowhere to check information back then. The Encyclopaedia Brittanica said nothing regarding ejaculating on roller coasters. My parents would have been horrified had I asked, and I couldn't ask my friends because, well, real men already knew these things.

I rode the same rollercoaster with my first crush Suzy Green a few weeks later, and I didn't ejaculate automatically, so I started shaking, which put the wind up Young Suzy. Afterwards, I explained the dicky logic — excuse the pun — to my parents and to Suzy's dad, who clearly wanted to murder me.

"Is an elf taller than a dwarf?" I ask John.

"Well, yes," he says. John is at least a certain percentage geek or nerd or whatever the politically correct term is, so I'm sure he's right about this. That Lord of the Rings guy is quite tall — Orlando Bloom.

"Why were you confused when your mother and father kissed?" I ask him.

"I wasn't *confused*," he says. "I just found it weird that my Dad was on his tiptoes. That's usually the woman's thing."

"Is it?"

"Well, isn't it?"

I look at my watch. We have been going six minutes with another twenty-four to go. I rub my face, and John opens his eyes and sits up.

"Hey, Doc. Do you think my peeping has something to do with my mother?"

"Why do you say that, John?"

"Well, I thought that since my mother left, there is no one in the world that loves me that way, and maybe I'm looking for love again by peeping in people's windows."

I sit up now and lean forward.

"No, John. You are getting confused because your mission involving your auntie, being the main case study today, has become *symbolic* of your pattern. You must understand that it is not the *pattern,* but a symbol. It's confusing that the size of both your aunties' and mother's breasts have come up in the same conversation and that your father being on his tiptoes is symbolic of you getting on your tiptoes and peeping through a window."

John straightens his back.

"That's amazing, Doc. You just *blew* my mind."

"No, John. These are *self-created* symbols born from your confusion and your brain's shortcuts. Our brains are like computers with large hard drives but weak processors, so, in the same process a computer uses, known as *dithering*, we take important snippets of information and surround it with assumptions based on past experiences. In other words, our gap in perception is filled with our past memories, which are themselves the partially assumed products of all the previous rounds of dithering."

John is lying down again.

"Are you with me, John?" I ask.

"Yeah, I'm here, Doc. Just trying to unpack what you said."

I'm still trying to unpack it myself. Sometimes the subconscious runs faster than the conscious.

We pause for a moment.

"When was the last time you had a girlfriend, John?"

"Me?" he asks, looking into his imaginary spreadsheet again.

I don't bother pointing out we are the only two here.

It's raining outside, and I stare out, considering the evening ahead — a cold drink and a good television show, maybe some noodles with extra preservatives, extra turkey and extra *loneliness*.

Most people don't consider the therapist's emotional path. They assume we can listen non-stop, even when the stories are tedious. But it's not like that. The therapist takes the ride *with* their client, and as I said, it's hard to hang around with these people and not feel a little dislodged. The whiskey helps by dulling the cynicism. It makes you care again — sort of.

"In college was my last proper girlfriend," he says. "I saw a girl last year, but we didn't do it or anything. We just hung out a bit, and then she said we should be friends."

"Do you still see this person?" I ask.

"No"

"How long did it last?"

"It was probably about two, maybe two and a half."

"Months?"

"No, *days*"

The situation is worse than I thought. The best thing for this man is to get laid. He has the money for a therapist, so why doesn't he get a prostitute? I'm almost certain it would be beneficial. I consider telling him, but it could open a whole new can of sour worms.

"Why don't you tell me about your *successful* missions, John?" I say. It's not a subject I have been keen to approach due to the risk of erection on my couch, but it's bound to come up at some point.

He begins his yarn like he is telling a Christmas tale under a tree with eggnog.

"The first time, it was a cold rainy night. It wasn't *technically* a mission as I had been to the Seven-Eleven to get some chocolate milk and crisps. I walked past this lovely house with a big white fence. The lights were on, so I stopped and pretended to make a phone call, pacing up and down outside and — "

"Wait, why were you *pretending* to make a phone call, John?" I ask.

"It's a good reason to hang around, Doc. You can't just *stand* there, or people will get suspicious. But people don't care about strange men speaking on the phone. If you ever see someone speaking on the phone and pacing up and down in the street, there is a good chance they are *peeping*."

This is fascinating. I write in my notepad — *Keep an eye out for strange men pacing on the phone*. The way things are going, I could end up being John's apprentice.

"Any open window with a light on can have me glued like an insect in one of those sticky traps," he says. "If a woman appears in the window, it's game over. This was one of those times. She had a towel around her head like a turban and another towel around her body. I dropped my chocolate milk, tried to pick it up and dropped my crisps. I grabbed them and stood up, looking between the wet picket fence. She disappeared, and when she came back, the towel had gone from her body. She had quite a hairy bush, and she was quite skinny. Her breasts were very perky, Doc, like two ski jumps."

I'm visualising Eddie the Eagle sliding down a pair of breasts and John's bloodshot eye jammed between two wet picket posts with an armful of groceries.

"Sounds like a pretty successful mission, John," I say, examining his crotch for signs of erection from a distance.

"Yes, but as I said, Doc, it wasn't a mission, just an accident," he says. "Which meant *three* problems for me. One, I couldn't see because my eyesight went blurry. It happens when I get too turned on. I wondered for a long time if it was why masturbation is supposed to make you blind. I would wake up in cold sweats and turn the light on to make sure I could still see. This was when I was masturbating probably eight to ten times a day."

"Sure, John," I say. "Am I right in assuming you aren't doing it that often anymore?"

"Correct, Doc. I'm down to *five* sessions a day. One in the morning, one at mid-morning tea after my coffee and biscuit, one about an hour after lunch, one at four pm when the neighbour gets home, one after dinner, usually around seven pm, then either once or twice before bed to help me sleep."

"I believe that's six or seven times, John, not five."

"Is it? Well, it's still less than what I was doing when I got paranoid about my eyesight. I wondered what was the most anyone had masturbated in a row. I looked it up in the Guinness Book of Records, but *nothing* was there. I called the Guinness Book hotline and told them my plan, but they hung up on me. I called a few more times, and I thought maybe it was too *risky* for the average punter, so I gave up and went for the *unofficial* record. On day one, I managed three in a row. The first was easy. The second one took a bit more work. I broke a sweat and got the old ticker going quite a lot. I must say, Doc, that third one was tough. *Nothing* turned me on anymore. I had to concentrate very hard. It took twenty-six minutes. By the end, I was drenched head to toe in sweat. It wasn't blissful like a regular orgasm. It was more like a sharp pain. I was a bit concerned about that. Afterwards, I passed out and slept for about twenty-four hours. A week later, I tried again and did *four* in a row. The fourth one took forty-five minutes. When I finally orgasmed, I ejaculated blood. So, I gave up on the record after that."

I shake my head and try to forget what he said. We need to get back on track.

"John, you mentioned there were three problems with the mission. The first being that your eyesight was blurry."

"Oh yeah, that was the *first* problem," he says. "The *second* problem was that I still had the phone to my ear, pretending to talk and pacing up and down to seem inconspicuous. With the other hand, I had my choc milk and crisps. So, I had no hand free to get at my dong, which was torturous. My *third* issue was that I was in the middle of a public street. It wasn't particularly well-lit, but still, you *can't* go getting your dong out in the street. It's too risky, Doc. It didn't last too long, anyway. The curtains closed, and I got one last look. That led me to one of the other problems — once you get a hit, you can't leave that site alone. I started hanging around every night, so eventually, I had to move house."

"You moved house because you couldn't stop stalking the woman?"

"Not the woman Doc, the window, but yes. I moved a few hours away."

"Have you ever been back there since John?"

"Never".

"So you did the right thing, it would seem?"

"Yes, it was the right thing in hindsight. It was a real low point in my life, though. It made everything so much worse for me."

"I'm sorry to hear that, John."

I *do* feel sorry for him now. When that happens, I know I'm reaching my whiskey limit. Some therapists say it's good to have empathy, but I disagree. Too much empathy clouds the vision. I prefer anger because it is clearer. If I was sober, I wouldn't care about John. He is a grown man who spies on strangers in a sexual way. Modern society might even call him a predator.

I pause again and tap my pen on the desk a few times like I'm going over some complex system I learned at University.

"So what happened with the second successful mission John?"

I know I am drunk because hearing about the second mission appeals to me, and I'm embracing these perverted outings as *missions*. I open the drawer, and the whiskey speaks to me again. I pour another — slightly more than half — glass.

John is lying down with his eyes closed, and his eyebrows are dancing like he is in that dimly lit street watching Turban Lady.

I down the horrible spirit — simultaneously committing to it being the last of the working day.

He busts me with an excessive mouthful, and I swallow it quickly, which gives me a pain in the chest and a face like someone fingered my anus without consent.

"Am I a pervert, Doc?" John asks.

The answer is obvious, but I can't tell him. I'm a professional, so I have to give the clinical answer to questions rather than the emotional, human version. And, to some degree, it's simply a side-effect of being a man.

Men just *love* shanking.

"You're not a pervert, John," I tell him. "You are a victim of your circumstances. Your actions are a little *unusual*, but you seem quite normal to me. You are trapped in a cycle of desire. And are you the horniest human in the world? I'd say probably no. In fact —"

" In fact," he interrupts, "when you think about it, I'm not raping anybody, am I? There *are* rapists in the world and child molesters and flashers. Surely I'm not as bad as that, am I, Doc?"

I pause too long because the pain in my chest is still there, and I'm thinking about heart attacks. Is this a heart attack? Will I be relying on John to give me mouth-to-mouth resuscitation? I feel a panic attack coming on, so I lengthen my breath and cough a few times.

"Are you okay, Doc?" John puts his feet on the floor and braces himself as if to get up and help me. I stretch out my palm to tell him to sit down. The last thing I need is him touching me. I'm not dying. I don't need the Heimlich manoeuvre. I just swallowed an air bubble with my whiskey.

"I just swallowed an air bubble," I say in a croaky voice. I pour some water and open my top left drawer, which contains my Gaviscon.

"No, John, You aren't as bad as a rapist," I tell him once I have recovered. I consider telling him that peeping can be a gateway drug to rape, but I don't — because it's not true, and I would only be saying it to *punish* him.

"But that doesn't mean you shouldn't take responsibility for your actions, John," I say. "Only *you* can turn this around." I'm quite drunk now. I know this because I'm impressed with the sound of my own voice. "Why don't you tell me about your *second* successful mission, John?" I say.

He assumes the corpse position again and goes into his memories.

"Well, unlike the first that I told you about, the second was an *actual* mission with planning and everything, or at least it became that way."

"Sounds creepy," I say out loud.

"Sorry?" he says.

The problem with drinking too much too early is that the words meant for your head stray out of your mouth. Technically, I can't hold any emotional opinions about my clients, and every therapist I know will make a show of their ethical neutrality, but it's all a front. I can guarantee every evening at the dinner table, they all speak about their clients with their spouses over corned beef, and you can be sure they all have an opinion.

"I was asking if you are getting *sleepy*, John. Do you need a coffee or something?"

"Oh, okay. No, I'm good."

"Please go ahead, John."

"You see, Doc," John continues, "the issue is that it was too close to home. I reckon it might be why the whole thing escalated."

Memories, as we discussed already, aren't real at least half the time — not even close. You remember bits and pieces, but if you look closely, your memories are like a dramatic play that you put on to entertain your awareness. Also, every time you revisit a memory, you adjust it to fit in with the story of your life that you are manifesting at that moment. So, each time you view it, you move further from the truth. Though, it still *feels* authentic because you don't know any better. And I always have this in my mind when I listen to my clients. How much of it is real? And how much of it is the *show*?

"I used to be a normal guy," John says. "I had a job 'n all that. I'd watch TV in the evening, and I'd go to work in the daytime. It was alright. I still masturbated a lot, but not nearly as much. This one day, I was sitting having a cup of tea before work and looking out of my bedroom window when the curtains opened in the apartment opposite me, and a woman appeared in white underwear."

I'm half listening but also writing in my diary: *Remember to pick up whiskey and cereal. And, oh, milk, you bastard.* Nothing like a bit of shopping list self-loathing.

"Tell me about the woman John. Was she young, old?" I am interested in the woman, but I'm also trying to drag this story out as long as possible. I want to fill the last ten minutes of our appointment so I can see my final client and go home. Home is my sweet place where I can drink without being judged by deranged people.

"She was older," he says.

Once you have sat in enough therapy sessions, you get to know what words like 'older' mean. They mean *old*.

"She had big breasts, Doc, though not as big as Mum's or Auntie's. She had a bit of cellulite around the middle too. But she had a *look* in her eye."

"What do you mean by a look, John?"

"It's the ultimate Doc. When she *knows* you are watching, it completes the circle."

He is the Lao Tzu of the peeping universe.

"She kept giving me this glance like she knew I was there. She walked up and down in her bedroom, looking at random stuff as if she was exploring a stranger's room. Do you understand me, Doc? It's the type of thing people don't normally do. That's how I know she set it up. I already had my dong in hand, but I was dressed for work, and I knew I would be late if I got started. I was a standup citizen at that time. It was a good job, and I used to shower every day. But this woman, Belinda — I called her that after Belinda Carlisle — destroyed it all. She stripped off her bra slowly. I watched her boobs drop and bounce like two jellies. They looked so heavy, Doc, as if you could get knocked out by them. They were like big boxing gloves."

I visualise getting pounded by two oiled-up breasts, and I realise John is really affecting me now. It concerns me when I exhibit behaviours similar to my clients, but it's inevitable because we have the same ingrained tendencies in ourselves. It's also the danger of whiskey. You become too empathetic and merge consciousness with your client a little. Here I am, and it's happening again. The story is turning me on, as is the idea of getting punched by massive boobs. I need to get through these last six minutes unscathed.

"Her nipples were huge," he continues. "I'd only seen pink ones, but these were brown — a lovely shade of brown and smooth like flying saucers. I was so close to ejaculating but kept stopping because I wanted to get good value."

John has a clear erection. So do I, for that matter, although mine isn't public. There is nothing homoerotic about this since John sees me as a professional, and I'm not attracted to him in the least. Also, our erections are about different things.

I appreciate what he said about value. You don't need to be a peeping tom to understand shanking value.

"She sat down on the edge of the bed and slipped her knickers off slowly, kicking them off. Then she stood up and folded her bra and knickers onto the bed. That's another sign that I know she *knew* I was watching. People don't do that. Why would you *fold* your used underwear, Doc? Surely you'd throw it in the laundry or something, right?"

His words are insightful, but they highlight the problem of getting too deep in empathy once again. I'm wondering if he has planted a seed in my brain. Will I go home tonight and check all the windows across from my apartment? It's possible. But maybe I'm just drunk. Am I going to end up becoming John? I'm *ripe* for that kind of transformation.

"So she stood up and walked randomly around the room again," John says. "My heart was beating faster than ever, Doc and I wondered if masturbation is good for the heart. Surely it's a form of exercise. I felt like I was going to have a heart attack, and my eyesight was so blurry I could barely see. She stopped in front of the window and pretended to look at some piece of paper, and I thought, *no one reads papers naked*. People put on clothes before reading papers. *That's just a fact*."

I nod enthusiastically.

"This happened right at nine am. I should have been at work, but no way I could go after that. I kept staring, wondering how she would escalate the show next. Masturbation is the next logical step, right, Doc? It's not like she could get *more* naked. So I'm expecting her to get on the bed and masturbate, but she sits down and reads a book. She stays there for ages, and it's in the dark bit of the room, so I can't even see her that well. It's so disappointing. Meanwhile, I'm still pulling away, and another fifteen minutes have passed. Before you know it, I was there for an hour and a half."

John looks at me, expecting a response, but all I can do is smile my constipated smile without making eye contact.

"After that, I couldn't stop watching, Doc," he says. "I'd wake up in the morning, and the first thing I'd do was sit and stare for ages. It got harder and harder to get ready for work. One day I gave up and decided I wouldn't go to work anymore. I sat there and watched the window all day. That was the start of the whole thing."

I look at my watch with mixed feelings. I want to delve further into John's descent into masturbatory oblivion, yet simultaneously want him out of my office as soon as possible. I see him correctly for the first time as a young child, confused by his tiny father and maybe some sexual feelings for his mother. As a child, he wasn't much different to me — the kid who thought it was appropriate to shank on a rollercoaster. Children are easily confused. They don't understand things like sexual shame because those things are conditioned, not inherent.

We are not born with sexual shame. It's a post-Christian thing. It's not normal. And I don't know the solution to all this. Are we supposed to introduce children gradually to the pleasures of sex like the French do with red wine? I'm not suggesting we show them our 'dongs' for God's sake. I just mean we can educate them early.

It's hard to know the answers when you are a product of conditioned sexual shame yourself. Sex is the basis of all life on this planet, and while we continue to teach it as a shameful thing, people like John will always exist, playing out that shame in strange and concerning ways. I could sit here and judge him for hiding in soaking bushes trying to view his aunties' knockers. We can all sit here and judge him. But we're all the same. We might not all be peeping toms, but we've all got something — that collection of scat porn on the hard drive, or the time you shanked the dog off when you were drunk, or the time you spied on your sister in the bath. We all have something — *all* of us.

"That's it," I say. "Times up, John. Let's continue this next week, shall we?"

John stands up, and his erection sticks out. He bows at me with his hands pressed together like I'm a Zen Master, and his erection bows as well.

Before leaving, he turns around.

"Hey, Doc?"

"Yes, John,"

"Do you think I will ever be normal again?"

Whiskey or not. I genuinely feel sorry for him.

"*Sure* you will, John," I say.

When it comes to therapy, honesty is *not* always the best policy.

THE CEO

The door closes behind John, the professional voyeur, and I pour the rest of the whiskey into a glass that is now half full or half empty, depending on your philosophy.

I'm on the fence between professionalism and functional alcoholism, and I'm paranoid seven days a week from practising with fake credentials. It's a hangover from being young. You put things in place because you are too naive to care. You are fearless, like a god. No one tells you that you become more of a porcelain horse every day as you get older.

It's not like I'm on the verge of a breakdown or anything. I've done enough meditation to hold it together. I know that ultimately the best form of treatment is *silence*. Those isolation tanks are good for it. You spend enough time in silence, and eventually, everything stops. That's when the *real* healing begins.

Becoming one of those mindfulness experts is tempting. I might be into getting paid to sit there doing nothing and teach others to do the same. It's a real hustle for a therapist. But I'm not *that* far gone yet. I still *care* about my clients to a degree, and the mindfulness gig still feels a bit shifty to me. Who am I to 'train' somebody for money? It's not about morals. You need to see deeply into someone to know what is best for them in that way. My vision isn't deep enough for that, and what is suitable for one person is totally wrong for another. It's too easy to get it wrong and screw someone up.

Therapy isn't that much different, but at least we have models, and it's *not* about spiritual development. It's about waking up in the morning without wanting to punch your wife in the face or throw yourself off a bridge. Those things are important. We all have our Suzy Greens — those rollercoaster ejaculations — moments of shame that we push deep down inside. Digging them up and assimilating them is the real work.

There's a louder-than-usual knock at the door.

"Just a moment," I say, throwing the empty Macallan bottle into the bin under my desk. I take a large chug of the golden petrol and slip it into my drawer. John, the professional voyeur, is *easy* to fool, but this is different. I flip a tiny mint from a dispenser into my mouth and chew on it.

"Come in".

Dana is the CEO of a HR company in the city. I know this because she told me last week during our first session. One of the issues I have with her is that I find her very attractive. Yet so much of what she told me last week was about getting sexually harassed by sticky men in the workplace. As her therapist, I'm not meant to be one of them. I'm meant to be this impartial professional whose only interest is her psychological health. Yet *here we are*. It's an appalling conflict of interest.

"Good Morning, Dana," I say, trying not to glare at her tremendous thighs.

"Hi, Frank," she says in a husky tone, turning around and smiling at me with perfect white teeth. "How are things with you?"

I mutter something about things being just fine.

She removes her jacket, lies on the couch, and straightens her short grey skirt. The combined effect of my session with John and half a bottle of spirit is affecting me. My heart is racing like I'm John glaring at Belinda and tossing himself off.

I need to get a grip. I feel like I have taken Viagra, and I truly hope my face isn't flushing red like one of those snow monkeys in Japan.

I think of my Grandma wearing lycra and doing squats which is my standard sexual antidote. But I take it too far, and soon Granny is being pounded by Dwayne Johnson with my Grandpa the cuckold shanking and filming the whole thing on a super 8mm camera. Dwayne turns into Christopher Walken having sex with my Grandma. I hear his voice, "Oh, Granny, you are so sexy," and I laugh out loud.

"What's so funny then, Frank?" Dana asks without looking at me. She is so direct. I like that about her. But a good therapist needs to cut through their thoughts constantly because thoughts get in the way of good therapy.

"Just something my last client said," I tell her. "My apologies." I clear my throat and move over to the comfortable chair opposite her while trying not to appear sleazy. With John, I stay behind my desk because I want to be as far away from him as possible. But this is different. I hear him directing me. *If you get in the chair opposite Frank, but seventy degrees left, you can tilt your head and* — I convince myself I'm not moving to get a better view up Dana's skirt, but the custard-cream-cargo-panted devil on my shoulder knows that's just *not true*.

"So where were we last week, Dana? I believe you had just started to work as a recruiter?"

"No, Frank. I had just moved in with Jack."

Jack was her fourth serious boyfriend.

"Of course," I say.

She sniffs a half laugh and opens the top button on her shirt. I'm not sure *why* she does that. Does she *know* I'm trying to see up her skirt?

I shake my head. *Get a grip on yourself, Man.*

"Jack was insatiable," she says. "All he wanted was to have sex. For the first three months, it's *all* we did. He worked as a car mechanic, and he would come home in his overalls, all sweaty and covered in grease. I usually sat on the sofa smoking bongs all day, and he supported me. He was so sweet in some ways. It became like a ritual. He would come home and lie on top of me on the sofa, and we would have sex like that every day without fail. Then we would eat something. He would have some bongs, and we would watch television, go to bed, fuck again, go to sleep, then wake up again and do the same thing."

I keep my legs crossed tightly and try to clear my thoughts, but it's no good. I'm in one of John's sticky insect traps, and I want to keep her on the subject of sex. Maybe I'm one of those sick male bastards from her office, but at least I'm aware. I'm a self-aware creep. Does that make me a bad person? I don't think humans are bad people necessarily. Our cravings are just stronger than our morals. Or maybe that's an excuse for *unreasonable* behaviour. I don't know.

"So you weren't working at that time?" I ask. It's a meaningless token question.

"Not at all. I would smoke bongs, watch TV, listen to music and masturbate a lot. You know what it was like back then, Frank. There was nothing to do in those times. It's not like there was an internet."

"Okay, so if there was no internet, what sort of stuff were you masturbating over?" My face burns, and I *know* it's flushing red as I ask — those damn snow monkeys. I raise my eyebrows and point my pen to bring an air of professional curiosity to what is genuinely a perverted attempt to have her talk dirty to me. She seems to take it *okay*.

"Well, *you* know, Frank." She sits up on the couch and looks at me. Her confidence is overwhelming. "We used our imagination, mostly." Her voice is softer, and she laughs. "I did have this one VHS. It was called *Two Guys And One Hole*."

My eyesight has gone blurry. I can't see properly.

"I think I wore that tape out," she says. "But I was twenty years old, and I was unstoppable. I had no toys, so I mostly stroked my clit. Sometimes I fucked myself with my fingers or various household items. Sometimes I used fruit."

I don't want to interrupt her flow, so I don't say anything. Instead, I lean forward in my chair and pretend to scribble more notes. She looks out of the window, and I look up her short grey skirt, desperately hoping for a glimpse of underwear, but I just see the darkness of my own empty soul.

I need some water, for *God's* sake. We are five minutes in, and I'm falling apart like a teenager. The default mindset for a male here is to think that she is purposely turning me on and that she wants to have sex. But I've been here too many times to assume that my evaluation of female psychology is correct. After years of counselling women, I still get it wrong almost every time. It's more likely she is opening up this way, assuming that I'm a professional and that I delved further into her masturbation habits for a *professional* reason. It pains me to change the subject, but I have to. I feel the presence of the perverted devil on my shoulder, and I can't afford a complaint. I've just got *too much* to lose.

"So, was Jack good to you?" I ask.

"*Fuck* no." Her answer is swift. There is a touch of anger and surprise in there too.

I nod without saying anything.

"The first six months were great. We fucked three times a day, and he supported me. But then the abuse started. First, he would make some remarks. He would call me a lazy bitch and then laugh as if it was a joke. I didn't think much of it because we often slagged each other off as a thing. But the smile as he said it got smaller and smaller. One day he said I needed to get a job. I was fine with that, but the way he went about it was so aggressive. He drank more and more. I know it sounds cliche, but he came home and raped me one day. It wasn't like I wasn't going to fuck him anyway. I didn't even say no. But it's like he wanted me to resist, and he hurt me to try to get me to resist."

My erection has gone now. I've never heard of rape described as cliche before, and there is still a look of humour on her face.

"And did the rape happen often?" I ask.

"No, that was the only time. I often wonder if he had been on something else that day besides the booze. We didn't have sex for some time. He became less interested and stayed out later and later until he would be coming home after midnight each night and passing out. That was when I got my first recruitment job."

I need to piss but don't want to interrupt her flow, so I'm jiggling my right leg.

Dana is lying down again. Her skirt has ridden right up, and I get a flash of knickers. I write the colour and material in my notepad — *red lace* — followed by the word *surprising*.

She instantly pulls her skirt down as if she is reading my mind.

"Would you excuse me for a moment, Dana?" I ask.

There is a tiny bathroom hidden behind a wall in my office. I stare into the metal basin as my piss hits the surface. It's difficult to piss with an erection. I have to bend over until I'm almost horizontal over the toilet and force my cock to point downwards like I'm pumping beer from one of those British beer taps. It takes effort to do that and *not* make a piss racket with Dana next door.

I have that washed-out drunken toilet sensation. I'm swaying as I finish, and I shake my cock like I'm developing a Polaroid. I wash my hands with fragrance-free pure Castile soap. You never know if some rose-scented crap might trigger a client's memory. One minute they're washing their hands, the next, they are in their memories, getting touched inappropriately while doing a jigsaw at Uncle Rico's house. So it's good to keep it neutral.

I apologise to Dana. She is sitting up now and staring out the window with one leg up on the couch. I drink some water and offer her some, but she shakes her head.

"Tell me about the job," I say, finishing a full glass of water. I feel fresh and professional.

She stares out of the window.

"It was pretty basic at first. I got an entry-level job as a Resourcer, which meant finding candidates for roles. The Account Managers were on a good thing. Clients would give them jobs, and I would do all the legwork to find people."

She swings around, places both feet on the floor and leans forward as if we are old friends. The idiot in me wants to kiss her. Obviously, it's a delusional idea. I'm supposed to be a professional, but more importantly, as I said, our misunderstanding of female psychology gets us into all kinds of trouble. Take John, for instance. I was trying to get him to orgasm quicker so he didn't fall down these rabbit holes. It's what I need to do now as I gaze into her green eyes — have a good shank — not in a perverted way, though. It's the only cure for my ailment. It's the sexual fire extinguisher.

"I would pretend to be other people," she says, laughing. "I would say I was from the candidate's HR department. Sometimes I even pretended to be a cop or calling from a hospital. These gatekeepers are impenetrable, you see. Gatekeepers are the secretaries and assistants who get harassed by recruiters all day. So they rarely put you through to a candidate. Candidates can read great on paper but tracking them down is only half the skill. You've still got to get them on the phone somehow and convince them to come and interview for a job with your client instead. I was committing fraud to speak to these people, and I finally realised that the most effective way was to fake an emergency — I might have a drink if that's okay, Frank?"

I jump to attention, pour her a glass of water, and nearly ejaculate in my underpants as her little finger brushes my hand during the handover.

She takes a few sips and puts it down.

"So, there's this young guy who is a master developer with some *rare* coding language, and he is one of only two of them in the whole city. *Everyone* wants this guy, and he gets hassled all the time, so no gatekeeper is putting you through, and no one, aside from his current agency, is getting hold of his mobile number. So what do I do? I call his office and tell them it's Doctor so and so from this particular hospital and that I need to speak to him urgently. Next thing I've got him on the phone sounding panicked. I deny the emergency, insisting that they must have misheard me. I know I'm against the clock, so I flirt as hard as I can and convince him to have a drink with me. That night I meet him, offer him more money and give him hope that we might fuck at some point. It's easy to work with nerds."

"And do you sleep with him?" I ask.

"No, Frank," she says, rolling her eyes. "I'm not a fucking hooker".

I could point out that she uses her sexuality to make money, but I don't. I'm the therapist here, and that means honesty around patterns, but my erection voids my right to point out just about anything. I'm applying a framework of morality, and I don't judge her actions at all, but I want to *look* like I'm judging her because I want to prove that I'm not just another dumb, manipulative man trying to get in her pants, which I am. It doesn't make sense, and it all comes down to the fact that I fancy her like crazy.

"I know, Dana. I didn't mean to imply you were a prostitute and — "

" But I get what you are saying," she interrupts. "Am I meant to feel bad about it, though? It's hard for a woman to get by in this world, Frank. Twenty years ago, it was much harder. Men use their sexuality and power all the time, and no one blinks an eye."

"I agree."

"So why shouldn't I be able to?"

"You should. I mean, you *can*."

She stares at me again for a minute.

"Do you want to fuck me, Frank?" she asks out of nowhere.

I'm trying to keep a straight face and not smile like a Cheshire creep. Is it a trap? How am I supposed to answer this? Is she offering to have sex with me, or is she just asking whether I *want* to? Does she want me to say yes or no? I try to get a read from her face, but there's nothing. She is brilliantly neutral — the sign of an experienced negotiator. For a moment, I wonder if she asked the question or if I heard it in my head or if she asked something different.

"Could you repeat that, Dana?" I ask in my most professional voice.

"Never mind," she says, flashing me her surprising red lace knickers for almost a whole second. I'm in pain, and I can't take it. I might have to ditch her as a client. Then maybe I could ask her out to dinner. Or I could climb on her right now and —

"I did well at that job," she continues as if nothing happened.

It's killing me that we move on. It's probably for the best, but I can't help but wonder if that was my one good opportunity.

"So they promoted me. I was an Account Manager in three months. No one at that business ever moved up that quickly."

"Oh yeah?"

"Yes. So now I had to find my clients of my own, which was even more of a blast."

She unbuttons her blouse a bit more. Once again, there is no reason for her to do that. The air conditioning is working fine.

"I'd find an advertised job and make up the ideal CV to go with the role. Then I would apply for the role and call myself Maria Taktarov — a highly sought-after programmer. Sometimes I would go under my desk, push right up against my computer and tell them I was in the server room."

"So, did you know about programming?"

"No, I did not, but neither did the dumb recruiters I spoke to. I knew enough words, and I would fill the gaps with Star Wars or Star Trek words. I would say things like *The Millennium Falcon Project*, and they would believe me. I would make up gibberish so complicated that they had no choice but to go along with it so they didn't seem like idiots. Anyway, they would set up an interview with Maria, but she wouldn't turn up. Then, I would call the client while they were still pissed off and offer them my perfect candidate instead. Once they were happy, I would take the client out for drinks, and some of them I did fuck. But not for the money — just because I felt like it."

She sits up again and smiles at me.

"Do you want to get a drink with me later, Frank?"

I smile, look at the floor and back up at her again. Of course, I can't go out with her. I'm a professional with a reputation to keep. If it gets out that I drink with my clients, I will never work in this town again. Then there are the plain old ethical considerations of it. She is my client, and it is my job to help her, not that I *know* how to help. So far, I haven't offered anything. All I have done is listen to her sweet voice and try to look up her skirt.

If anything, she has issues with the males in her life, always thinking she slept her way to the top and that, therefore, she will sleep with them too. It's some bizarre method when the therapist role-plays the very problem he is trying to fix. It would be weird and unethical to say yes. It is absolutely out of the question.

"I'd love to, Dana," I say.

· · · · ● · ● · · ·

I get to the place at about nine-thirty.

After Dana left, I went into my tiny bathroom and had a medicinal shank. I looked up her profile on LinkedIn, dropped my pants and sat down on the metal seat, pulling myself off with the energy of a teenage Rubik's cube champion. I moved on to a YouTube video of her at a conference in a small black dress. The internet in my office is poor, so it kept cutting out. Finally, I just thought about seeing her red knickers, and that was enough.

After that, I went home and napped for an hour or so. Then I ordered some ribs and had a cold shower. I stuck on my most acceptable blue shirt and headed out to meet Dana at this classy bar.

She offers her cheek for me to kiss, and I oblige.

"You seem different outside of the office," she says. Her legs look unbelievable.

"Different, how?" I ask as the bartender comes up. I order vodka, lime and soda. I want nothing to do with whiskey after this afternoon.

Dana is drinking a Martini. Why would she drink anything else?

"I don't know," she says. It's the first time I have noticed a degree of girlish shyness in her. "You look *attractive*, that's all."

I try to suck the blood away from my face. At least my erection is controllable now since my late afternoon jerk-off session.

"I know I shouldn't say this as your therapist, but you look unbelievable."

She does look unbelievable in that dark blue velvet dress. It's short, with thin straps. She has an incredible tan, and her shoulders are covered in freckles that I want to eat like M&Ms.

"No, you shouldn't say that, Frank. For fuck's sake. Are you trying to make things complicated or what?"

She laid out a carpet for me, and I walked along it like a naked emperor. Then she tripped me over, spread my arse cheeks and had the whole crowd laughing and throwing fruit at my yellow-stained sphincter. She's like a goddamn sorceress. I feel myself slipping further into her grasp, and it's killing me.

I know that strength is an attractive quality. Years ago, a mentor said to me, *let them come into your world, don't go into theirs.* But that's easier said than done as a therapist. If someone like

John can affect me with his world, how much easier is it for a goddess to suck me in?

I'm a man, and we are weak bastards. They say that the second brain resides in the stomach, but the third brain lives right in the head of the penis for men. I thought about writing a paper on it once called *The penis is alive, and it's a real mean prick*.

My drink arrives. I shake my head and swallow half of it quickly. I can feel her glaring at me, and the childish school-boy in me wants to leave. I'm hurting badly, but I can solve this by walking away and ditching her as a client.

"I'm just teasing Frank," she says, putting her hand on my hip.

I'm a strong, confident man. I don't need this shit. Why am I feeling like one of those geeks that she manipulates for her job? I look up, and she is smiling at me with perfect teeth. I'm not up for marriage, but I could marry this woman. I'm generally a dominator in the bedroom, but I would happily get whipped by her. She could make me wear her knickers. She could do me with a strap-on for all I care.

"Tell me about yourself, Frank," she says, taking a sip on her martini and eating a tiny pretzel out of the dish on the bar.

"You shouldn't eat those snacks, you know. They say — "

" I know, Frank," she interrupts. "You're going to tell me they are covered in piss and semen and all of that. It's a fairly predictable thing to say. Have you considered that some people might like to eat those things?"

"What, piss-covered pretzels?"

"Semen-covered pretzels, Frank. You know about my past. You know I'm a slut. Why wouldn't I want to eat semen?"

This is why therapists don't date their clients. The rules are there for a reason. She has thoroughly hypnotised me. I'm doomed.

I signal the bartender to get me a double, and we sit in silence, watching him make and deliver it. This isn't going well at all. I'm right back in front of Suzy Green and her parents.

"Would you like another drink, Dana?" I ask, attempting to regain control like a weak-kneed boxer on the ropes. My self-preservation is ready to throw in the towel while my cock-brain drives on like Rocky Balboa.

"I'm *fine*," she says, lighting a cigarette and turning away from me. She crosses her legs and smiles at another guy across the bar. He looks like a young Mickey Rourke with tattoos and a mullet, and he is interested. Why wouldn't he be? She is *unbelievable*.

It hurts that she is ignoring me now. I have been a therapist for decades. I know what she is doing, but I can't stop getting pulled along by her games like a puppet. Somehow I need to stop desperately trying to get her attention. I need to be the strong cowboy, not one of her coder geeks.

"You can't smoke in here, damn it," I say, channelling Bogart in Casablanca or whatever. I'm not really into old movies, but I'm fairly sure they were dominant, womanising bastards. It's a risk. I know that. And as the words come out, I instantly regret it because I don't sound like an old movie star. I sound like a controlling prick because this *isn't* the fifties.

"Fuck you, Frank," she says, standing up. She blows smoke in my face, puts the cigarette out in the pretzels, picks up her handbag, and walks out of the bar. The way she does it is *classy*.

Just about the whole place is staring at me now. Of course, they are assuming I was a prick to *her*. Maybe I was, I don't know. I mean, you *can't* smoke in bars anymore. Wasn't I simply performing my duty as a citizen? I've got John the Voyeur on my shoulder, and he's shaking his head at me, saying, *No, no, no,* like Newman in Jurassic Park. He's right. I tried to dominate her, and it failed.

· · · · · · · · · ·

I thank the cab driver and get out a few blocks from my apartment to walk in the fresh air. It's raining, and the city lights are sparkling like jewels in the puddles. I think about John the Voyeur, and I realise a degree of admiration for him — not for his stinking antics but for his dedication to the field and his authenticity. He knows who he is and doesn't try to put on a show for others. He doesn't hold down a day job as a fraud. He quit his job to peep full time. He is following his passion.

Not me. I'm still pretending to be a therapist. I wonder if I'm even helping John or any of my clients. For decades I have been building more confidence in my abilities. I have justified my lack of real education with a disdain for the system and by saying that the world is in such turmoil that we can't be doing therapy right. I never doubted myself for years, but now I doubt myself every day. Some might say it's part of the process. Do we need that self-doubt to keep questioning our methods? Is that how we go deeper? I wonder what that bastard Freud would say about all this?

Well, what would you say about it, Freud, you bastard?

I shouted that last bit out loud, and now a young couple are crossing the road to avoid me. I want to explain that ordinary people shout out to God during their breakdowns, while therapists shout out to Freud. Never mind, they wouldn't understand.

Surely the truest moment in life is right before death because there is nothing left that is worth the pretence. We're all decaying leaves, and that's a bitter pill to swallow. Why are we so ashamed of our own suffering that we have to pretend it's not happening?

It's a beautiful night. I think about Dana again. Maybe *she* is the therapist, and I'm the patient. After all, isn't this where we were heading at one point in our session? She built a career around manipulating men. Then, after she has beaten them all, they *still* treat her as inferior — even those way below her. Maybe she —

"Dana," I say out loud. She is standing out the front of my apartment block, leaning against the wall and smoking a cigarette. "How do you know where I live?"

She flips herself off the wall, walks up to me, takes another drag of her cigarette, drops it and puts it out with her foot.

"It's what I do, Frank. I find out information."

"I thought you slept with people for money," I say without breaking a smile.

"It's what we all do, Frank." She presses her lips against mine.

I'm done trying to be the prick cowboy — the old sexist movie star. Whatever she wants, I'm in.

She pulls back again and looks into my eyes. Now she is grabbing my skin through my shirt, and it's painful, like getting one of those cow bites as a kid, but I won't show weakness. I grab her hand and pull her towards the glass doors. I unlock the gate fast, and we fall into the jarring white foyer. I press the elevator button, and it lights up green.

Ting.

We're in the elevator now. I press the number six, and the door closes. She slams me against the wall and undoes my belt. The door opens too soon, and a Betty White-looking character stares at us. We run past her, laughing like teenagers. My loose belt rings like I'm Santa Claus coming up the corridor.

Merry Christmas, neighbours.

I open my apartment door faster than I ever have and close it even faster. She tears open my fly like a packet of Doritos. Then she yanks my underpants down, aggressively grabbing my cock with her teeth and lips, drooling all over it, sucking it hard. It's *unbearable.*

I'm leaning against my kitchen bench, and I notice the plate left over from my ribs, which I forgot to soak. It's embarrassing that I left this sticky sauce to harden on a plate.

She squeezes and yanks on my nuts so hard that they might burst. Her sucking is now industrial level, like my cock is stuck in one of those commercial vacuums — the type they use in offices. I think she might suck it right off. I can't take it, and I *know* I will blow at any second.

I think about John in the rain watching his Auntie. I think about him getting an erection on my couch, but it's not working. I look down at Dana's glistening midnight hair and tell her to stop, but she won't.

"Dana, I'm going to blow. Please *stop,*" I shout.

She pulls off with a smacking sound and stands up.

"Where's the bathroom?" she asks.

We go to the bedroom, and she goes into the bathroom. I'm thinking that I need to ditch her as a client tomorrow. This is far from professional. I hear Dana pissing, and I do that cliche breath check thing. My breath smells like an arsehole, but I can't find my mints. Too late, the toilet flushes and the door swings open.

"Did you think about me after I left today, Frank?" she asks.

Why bother being a pathetic lying bastard? I don't care anymore. I need to be more honest — more like John the Voyeur.

"Yeah, I had a wank, actually," I say.

She melts my brain again with that smile she does, and then she crawls over me like a lioness about to feed. I'm a goddamn antelope.

"And what sort of things do *you* masturbate over, Frank?"

So that's settled. She *did* know my game when I asked her that question. There was me thinking she was thinking that I was thinking that she thought I was asking a professional question. Like I said, I *always* get it wrong.

"I read people for a living, Frank," she says. "What did you expect? Why do you think I gave you great details about how I finger myself?"

She pulls her velvet dress over her head, revealing her unearthly body dotted with freckles and a lace green two-piece. She puts one hand around my throat, squeezing gently and spreading her legs. She pulls her knickers to one side and slides my cock, still soaked with her saliva, into her. I ask her mentally about *protection,* and I get no reply. Then she squeezes my neck tighter and pulls me deep into her.

It's tight, and I know I'm not going to last. It squeezes all the blood right in and out as she slides up and down.

She leans forward and whispers in my ear.

"What were you wanking over, Frank?"

Everything felt good. I was beyond lying.

"It was your LinkedIn Profile," I say.

She pauses, takes her hand off my throat and creases up with laughter. I feel a burning sensation in my forehead. I'm young, confused and desperately in love with Suzy Green, but I've just lost her forever through my own shameful actions. The whole world is laughing at me. But she leans forward again, kisses my lips and rides me slowly but forcefully.

I'm Jack, her fourth serious boyfriend, and she is Suzy Green. And together, we fuck away the shame.

· · · · · ● · ● · · ·

I wake up to a horrible alarm and a sore cock.

Dana is gone, but her green lace knickers aren't, and I wear them on my face for a minute or two, snorting her hot pussy atoms and blowing in record time. What's the number for the Guinness Book?

After my shower, I'm standing in the kitchen making coffee and texting her:

Did you leave early? Want to have dinner tonight? F

Am I being pathetic? I fill a bowl with muesli and sit at the bench. There is a document there. It's a position description:

CLINICAL PSYCHOLOGIST
MARSDEN AND WELLS CLINIC
DANA REED AGENCY
175–190K PA

On the top of it, there is a yellow sticky note.

Have a look, Frank. No pressure. Great opportunity for you — more pay, especially. How about dinner Monday to discuss? Thanks for last night. Dana x

I feel sick.

THE ROCK STAR

I *was* cut up about Dana.

I'm not anymore. I realise the job gives me something over her. It means she'll be back, and I'll take my time, talk to her about the job and have sex with her at least one more time. Maybe she'll fall in love with me? Then again, why would she fall in love with me? Besides, why would I want to be with her? There's *no way* I could put up with her sleeping with her clients, so if I'm with her, she would have to choose between me and her career.

That's better. *Bogart.*

Controlling bastard, more like. I've been around enough pathetic creeps to know that it's unattractive to a woman. It would be better if she kept doing what she was doing, and I was just someone who gave her a big commission once. I'll take the job — not yet, but at some point. She will get me. She is too good.

It's Monday morning now, and I'm staring at the fresh bottle of golden petrol on my desk like I'm on some quiz show called, '*Who wants to be an alcoholic?*'

No need to phone a friend, though. I know the answer. I *do* want to be an alcoholic. Why not? I am sick of the inner debate. Sure, it's morning, but what's the difference?

The booze doesn't care, and neither do I.

I've seen the other side of the coin, too, though. Alcoholics *don't* want to be alcoholics, and that saves me in some way. It's like the idea of oblivion as an escape from the pain of life. Is it better to be alive and in pain or to be nothing? If suicide is being used to counter mental pain, it's a high-risk plan since there is no proof that the mind does not continue after death. Sure, I wasn't brought up in a war zone or sexually abused, so it's easy to say. But there is one thing I have learned from listening to people's horror stories — it is our *own* ropes and our *own* knots that tie us to our past.

So why can't we just ditch the past completely instead of trying to resolve it? What happens then? Madness? How can I know anything without relating it to the past? Can I even function without my past? Is it possible to be happy *and* mad? Is madness only torturous if you want it to make sense?

There's a gentle knock, and I check my watch. It's 9.04 am.

I sigh and reluctantly put the bottle to bed in my top drawer and pour some water.

Come in, you bastard.

He tells me his name is Robson, and I don't know why since I've listened to his music for years. I take from his pseudonym that he wants this session to be anonymous. And why do rock musicians always wear cowboy boots and sunglasses everywhere?

"How are you, Robson?" I say. It's like the mantra of the therapist. It's a dumb opener. But I'm pathetically feeling a little starstruck.

He pouts and sits down like a frail pensioner on the edge of the couch. There's maybe an inch or two supporting his tiny, bony arse.

He stares out the window as if I've asked him the meaning of life.

"Ah fuck it, I'm alright," he says in a voice like Keith Richards to anyone outside of London. He pauses again, leans back on the couch and pulls out a cigarette.

My first instinct is to tell him he can't smoke here, but I've been there before. Someone said that the definition of insanity is doing the same things and expecting different results. That's nonsense. It's not the definition of insanity, but it's still not advisable.

"Can I have one of those, Robson?" I say instead.

Robson jumps up with the enthusiasm of a man desperately seeking comradeship.

I haven't smoked for twenty years, but it might be a good substitute for my descent into alcoholism.

I press the button on my desk, and it makes the usual high-pitched buzz like a distressed ferret.

FFEEERRRTTT

"Janice, can you fetch me a couple of ashtrays?"

Silence.

"I'm sorry, what?"

"Ashtrays, Janice, I need a couple of ashtrays."

"Well, I don't think we have any ashtrays."

"Okay, well, can you get some, please? Nice ones — crystal if you can."

Janice gives a confused *okay*, and I take two water glasses, placing one next to Robson on the table and one on my desk as temporary ashtrays.

The cigarette is rough. It's a Marlboro which has the same horrific taste it had when thirteen-year-old-me first smoked while camping in a friend's garden. I know from experience that you can get used to that flavour. With perseverance, it's possible to enjoy smoking again. And it's got to be better than alcoholism.

"So what brings you here, Robson?" I ask with the embarrassing cough of a novice smoker.

"Well," he says, rubbing his forehead and squinting his yellow eyes.

"I caught herpes when I was twenty-four. The bird was nice and that, but it burnt like a fuckin bastard. Now I have to wear these fuckin tight leather pants for my job, and fuck Pal, I can tell you when you've got an outbreak, it's like someone is trying to burn your fuckin cock off with a fuckin flame-thrower."

These first sessions often take time to get going.

"Go on," I say. I'm intrigued, but I want more cigarettes, so I press the ferret button again.

FFFEEEERRRTTT.

"Janice, can you get me a packet of thirty Marlboro while you are getting ashtrays?"

"As in the cigarettes?"

"Yes, Janice, Marlboro cigarettes."

Silence.

"Hello?"

"You want me to go *now*?'

"Yeah, sure, why not. Take an early lunch."

"It's ten past nine, Frank,"

I let go of the button and shake my head.

"Can't get good staff these days, Robson."

He nods awkwardly.

"So," I remind him, "You had an inflamed knob,"

"Yeah, that's right. Thing is, I was fuckin a lot of girls back then too. I'm no supermodel, but they would fuckin throw 'emselves at me — rubbing their titties on me and fuckin sucking me off. Every night on tour, I would fuck at least two or three of 'em."

"Sounds like a good life Robson."

"It was to a fuckin degree, but you can't keep taking coke and Viagra every night, you know? Anyway, I'm in my fifties now, and I'm fuckin clean, but I can't stop thinking bout all the birds I gave herpes to."

"So you weren't using protection then?" I ask half-heartedly. My head is spinning from the cigarette, and I'm thinking about having sex with Dana again. I'm pinning her down on the bed and saying, *You want me to take the job, do you? Eh? EH?*

I realise I'm deep in thought and that Dana has broken me as a therapist. I can't stay present with Robson. I'm smoking like a devil. I need a shit badly because the nicotine has loosened my bowels. And I am doubting all of my abilities.

"What, you mean, rubber Johnnies?" he mutters. "Nah, Pal, except when —"

" You want a drink, Robson?" I interrupt, pulling the fresh bottle of Macallan from its bed. I'm not hiding anymore. I'm taking a leaf from the book of John — the book of *authenticity* along with whatever madness that may bring.

Robson sits up and stares at the bottle, silently mouthing words as if conversing with an old friend.

"I'm fuckin three years clean," he says. Then he claps his hands and rubs them together. "But yeah, go on then. Mundee mornin' innit?"

Mundee mornin' it is indeed. I should be panicking about my job right now, but I don't care anymore. I grab two more glasses from the back shelf, pour two large whiskeys and hand one to Robson. A part of me is bonding with him, but another part wants to punish him because he has a tiny arse and because I want to punish Dana and John, the Voyeur.

I'm no longer a therapist. I'm a distributor of *karma*. I am Yama, the Lord of Death, and I want to collectively punish my clients by offering a drink to an alcoholic.

I see myself doing this, and I wonder if I'm imploding or having a nervous breakdown. Surely I have to trust in the subconscious process. It doesn't *feel* like a selfish action, so it must be the process. The man is three years clean, though. How could having a drink possibly help him?

He downs the whiskey and holds it out again.

"Fill me the fuck up," he says. I down mine and fill them both up, sitting on the chair next to him.

He nods at me, holds up his glass and takes a sip.

"I'm sorry about your sobriety," I say.

"I'm not," he says. "It was going to happen sooner or later, Pal. You know fame isn't what it's cracked up to be, Doc. Shall I call you Doc?"

"Call me Frank, and yeah, I've heard that about fame. I like your music, by the way."

"Yeah, cheers, Frank."

"Shall I keep calling you Robson or — ?"

"Yeah, Robson's my real name, actually. The other one's just a fuckin stage name. I'm trying to get away from it. You know, there's a certain amount of fame you can get away from, but past a certain point, it's fuckin' impossible, Pal. There's no escape. Wherever you go on the earth, some cunt always wants something from you."

"So you're not enjoying the fame then, Robson? Did you enjoy it at one stage?"

"Oh yeah, in the early days, it was fuckin mental — chicks, drugs, rock n roll. It's the fuckin dream, Frank. But there's the other side, too, even at that point. People crave fame, but they don't see the other side — the pubic hair and razor blades in the mail, the *constant* stalking, the kids threatening to commit suicide if you don't fuck them. It's a fuckin shitshow, my friend. Then as you get older, your fuckin dick stops working, and all the fuckin drugs come back to haunt you. You get paranoid as fuck, then the depression comes, then the existential dread. A million fuckin ghosts all come to haunt you at once. You've been to Lucifer's brothel, bought the most expensive hooker, and now the demon pimp is coming to collect his fuckin cash."

"Jesus, Robson," I say as I top our drinks up.

"Good name for my solo project," he says, lighting another cigarette and offering me one. I accept.

"So, where are you at now?" I ask him. "Three years clean, eh? Again, sorry for offering you a drink."

I do feel genuinely sorry now.

"I'm going through a crisis myself, actually," I say.

"Oh yeah?" he says. "I guess being a shrink, you'd pick up on everyone's bollocks and feel like you're going fuckin mad after a while, wouldn't you?"

The bastard *nailed* it.

"Yeah, believe me, I've been around my share of crazy people in the rock n roll lifestyle, Son, and they rub off on you. And, no doubt, there's some fuckin *woman* involved, right? There always fuckin is. Having a dick is fuckin torture, Frankie."

"Are you married?" I ask, to change the subject.

"I *was* married until a year ago," he says. "That was my fourth marriage. I met her on tour like all the others. They get fascinated with you. You start off as their fuckin idol. Then they realise how fuckin dysfunctional you are, and they can't take it. Also, I fuckin cheated on each one of them many times. People can judge famous people for cheating on their wives and husbands, but it's hard, Pal. Imagine that thousands of women want to fuck you wherever you go with no questions asked. Don't matter if you ain't showered for a week or if you just ate a giant hot dog or just shit your knickers. They want to fuckin *do it*. Young ones, too, Frank. Fuckin *young* girls."

"I don't wanna know about that stuff, Robson."

"Nah, bullshit. You wanna know. It's a warning to you, so you don't get fuckin famous, Frankie. You know, we didn't think much of it. They wanted it. I wanted it. I used to ask them how old they were, and they always said fuckin eighteen, but they weren't — sometimes not even close. When you're that fucked up, Pal, you don't give a fuck. You don't worry about it till you become an old bastard — that's when that kind of shit tortures you. Not just the guilt, but the fear of being outed and ending up in prison getting reamed by some prick with love-hate on his fuckin knuckles. Every day, I want to relax but can't. Every night I can't fuckin sleep. People treat me like my life has been a success, but it's been one monumental fuckup after another. I'm full of fuckin regret and guilt, and I can't fuckin shake it."

I know I'm supposed to say something at this point, but I don't. I should probably tell him that every client I see believes their life is a series of monumental fuckups — but I *don't*. Instead, I stare at the burning cigarette in my hand and dump it into the glass. I look out the window. The sun has come out, and the sky is a perfect empty blue. A light beam catches Robson's crystal glass, sending a rainbow across the room. I take it as a sign.

"Robson, it's a beautiful day. Do you wanna get out of here?"

I see the old rocker's face light up. His wrinkles dissolve for a second, and I see the confident twenty-something come out.

"Yeah, I fuckin do, Frankie."

He pulls out an old flip phone and holds it to his ear.

" — yeah, I'm fuckin ready. Meet you out the front."

· · · · ●● · ● · · · ·

Why do I feel like I just walked into a *bender*?

We're in the back of a limo. Not one of the really long stretched ones but just a slightly stretched, very nice Lexus, with enough space to splay out and drink.

We're in Robson's world now, and he is digging around in a pouch in the back seat. Eventually, he pulls out a bottle of mescal.

"AHHHH, Frankie, my Old Pal," he says, slumping down next to me. "I've been saving *this* for a special occasion."

"Back on the drink, are we, Sir?" says this Michael Caine voice in the front seat.

"You got a fuckin *problem* with that?"

It's the first sign of aggression I've seen from Robson. Maybe he is an angry drunk. Maybe this wasn't the best idea.

"Not at all, Sir, just trying to stay in the loop."

"Good."

Robson doesn't bother with glasses now. He uncorks the mescal with a pop. Strangely, it's the same sound Dana's mouth made on my cock the other night. A third of the bottle disappears down Robson's gullet like it's Sunkist. Then, he hands it to me, and I take a long swig from the bottle.

"It's *spicy*," I say because it *is* spicy. It has a very strange taste.

Robson is staring out of the window and doesn't hear.

"Where are we going, Robson?" I ask.

He smiles like a true child of Satan.

"Bangkok," he says.

Hopefully, he is joking. I laugh a half-laugh, but he doesn't respond. He is staring out of the window again.

"Is that the name of some nightclub uptown?" I ask him, hopefully.

"Nah, it's the greatest fuckin city in the world," he says.

I've seen this situation before. People go to Bangkok because the laws are slippery there. You can have sex with young women or men or any variant of the two, and you can buy strong prescription drugs in your high street chemist. His response confirms my bender fears. I'm up for a bender, I just don't know if I'm ready for the *rock star* level of bender just yet.

"Well, I can't come, Robson," I say.

He swings around with the enthusiasm of a man who needs someone to go on a bender with. For a minute, I feel sorry for him, but it doesn't help my fear. I'm regretting this whole thing.

"I don't have my passport," I tell him.

"Let's go get it then, you fucker."

"No, I mean I don't *have a* passport. It's expired, I'm afraid. I need to organise a new one. It's going to take *weeks*." It's bullshit. The damn thing is sitting in my sock drawer at home. And Robson knows I'm lying by my facial expression of pure terror.

He stares me down, putting one hand on each of my shoulders.

"Look, I know you're fuckin scared, Frankie. Everyone's got their emotion of choice. Mine is guilt, and yours is fear. You spend your days trying to help people, but you don't realise you're sucking in all their shit. Then one day, you start drinking to deal with it. Before you know it, you're a fuckin train-wreck like all the other fuckin shrinks. You've got this wild side that's trying to get free, but you can't escape your job, so you bring it to work and end up dumping shit on your fuckin clients instead."

I've got a lump in my throat. No one has ever understood my life as deeply as this rock'n'roll bastard.

"I'm not qualified, Robson," I say spontaneously.

The old dog smiles and nods.

"You're a fuckin fraud?"

"Yep"

He laughs.

"Well, praise fuckin Caesar. Dr Frankie, the fuckin fraud. So your emotion of choice *is* guilt, then?"

"Indeed."

"We've got a lot more in common than I thought, Frankie. We are guilt brothers, my friend." He holds the Mescal bottle up. "Here's to booze and guilt."

I nod and cheers him with an invisible glass.

"Now, let's get your fuckin passport."

"Nah, I don't think so, Robson. Look, come to think of it, just let me out here, would you?"

"Ah, for fuck's sake Frankie. Pull over here, Mike, would you?"

The driver's name is Mike. If he is Michael Caine, I will know this is a dream — Robson, John, Dana, *all of it*.

"Yes, sir," he says, spinning around to face us. He's pale with a black moustache. Not Caine. Repeat, Not Caine.

Now we're getting out in this park, and it's hot, and I'm feeling the approach of *depression* in my mind. Clients have come to me to deal with it, and I try not to send them to a psychiatrist for the drugs, but they want it to go away *so* badly, and nothing will do it quickly enough. Meditation takes years, and what else is there?

I'm convinced it's a serotonin issue, but not a lack of it, more of a *transport* issue. There's always serotonin in the body, but not where it's needed. It hangs out all over the body. It's why exercise seems to increase serotonin. The increased heart rate unblocks the channels and allows for a more effortless flow of serotonin, oxygen and other resources. Ninety per cent of the time, anxiety and depression are transport issues. Still, that's considered an unorthodox opinion and not the kind that sells drugs.

I've been talking to Robson about this for twenty minutes, sprawled out on the grass. The mescal is empty, and the bottle of absinthe is a third down. The absinthe is all him. I'm too busy harking on about serotonin while Robson is drinking himself to death in the sun.

"You know," he says, "It's no surprise. I can be a boring prick, especially when I get drunk. Besides, absinthe ain't even hallucinogenic."

I'm not sure how any of that relates to serotonin.

"Oh yeah?" I say.

"Yeah. It's strong as a cunt, and it tastes like thrush, but it won't make you trip. Mushrooms, on the other hand — or acid, well. Different story, Pal. They make you fuckin *trip*, Frankie."

I'm not sure if he is even talking to me anymore or doing some alcoholic interview with an imaginary audience.

"You know, Frankie, I can get whatever drug I want delivered to me in half an hour, no matter where I am in the world?"

He *is* talking to me. But I've started thinking about Dana again, wondering if it is impossible for us to be in love. I mean, the sex was unbelievable, for me at least. Why leave the job description on the table? Was that a joke? Or is it her standard move? I don't know what I'm doing here with this wasted rocker. I should go and see her.

"It's a fuckin problem, you know?" Robson says.

"What is?"

"Twenty-four-seven drug delivery, Pal."

"Oh, right,"

Technically, we are still in therapy.

"You can't fuckin escape. It's a fuckin nightmare. Death is the only fuckin escape, you know?" Robson says.

His words aren't helping my depression.

Two young girls who can't be much older than sixteen arrive in our space.

"Oh my God," one of them says. "It's you. Oh my *God*."

"Yeah, it's me," I say with a childish grin, but they ignore me. They sit on either side of Robson and start stroking his face.

"Oh, that's fuckin nice, Frankie, yeah. Keep doing that."

"It's not me, you bastard," I say.

Robson is wasted, and I'm jealous of him. Life has given him everything on a golden plate, and all he wants to do is bitch about it.

I want to be stroked on the face by young girls. I want to tell them his name is Robson, and he has herpes, but I don't. I watch him lay there in despair as the girl starts fondling his cock through his jeans. He says nothing and I'm wondering if he is dead now.

"You alright, Robson?" I ask.

"Who said that?"

"It's me, Frank."

He hands me the absinthe, and I take a large gulp. Robson's description of this diabolical brew didn't come close. It's almost cruel how foul it tastes.

Michael Caine turns up from nowhere and says something so loud it makes me throw the Absinthe bottle. It hits the second girl in the chin, and she yelps, ducking down and covering her face.

"Oh, I'm so sorry," I say, but she says nothing. Maybe *she* is dead now.

I lean over a bit.

"Are you okay?" I ask her.

She lifts her head, smirks and kisses me on the lips. I get an instant erection, and I don't resist. I mean, she can't be more than sixteen, but I'm drunk, and —her head is *still* on the floor, and I'm *still* sitting up watching her, and the bottle of absinthe is *still* in my hand.

Did I just go back in time?

"She's fine," her friend says. "She's just having a lie-down."

"What is going on, Robson?" I ask him.

I think I'm having a breakdown of some kind.

"Nah, Pal," he says, sitting up and grabbing the absinthe back off me and taking a swig. "It's just the acid kicking in."

What does he mean by that? Did Robson take acid?

The first girl has Robson's cock out and is shanking him off fully in the open. I notice that his dick is *massive*. It's supernaturally big, or her hand is really tiny, and I can't tell which is which, and I start laughing. It feels strange to laugh. I haven't laughed in years, I don't think.

"Robson," I say.

"Robson," says one of the girls. It must be girl two, who is still lying head down on the ground. "*Who is Robson?*"

The first girl starts sucking Robson's cock, and it's making me *horny*.

"Yeah, who the fuck *is* Robson?" Robson says, laughing hysterically. He is so casual about getting his cock sucked. It must happen all the time.

"Help me up, would you? Let's go get a proper drink," Robson says. His face looks awful now. He looks like an old man, but his face is changing, and worms are coming out of his eyeballs. That can't be just the absinthe. Robson said it's not even hallucinogenic.

"Mike, what did you do? Did you put acid in my drink?" I say.

He looks like my *Dad*.

"My name is Robson," he says, laughing uncontrollably again.

I realise I called him *Mike*. I can't breathe. I feel paranoid all of a sudden. Nobody is around me. I am alone in the park, and I'm having an episode. Or maybe I'm *dying*. Is this death? Are these the hallucinations of the bardo Tony Robbins spoke about? Or that bastard monk who sold his Ferrari or whatever?

I feel hands on me from behind and nearly have a heart attack. Michael Caine helps me to my feet, and I see everyone ahead. "You're only supposed to blow the bloody doors off," I shout, creasing with laughter. I say it again and again, and I can't breathe. I look at Michael Caine's face, and it is not his. It's Borat's face. I'm trying to remember what Borat says, but all I can say is *Bloody*.

We're in the back of the limo again. Robson is sprawled out and sweating like a badger. He looks like a badger, too — a *giant badger*.

"It'll put you back where you're meant to be," he says with his eyes closed.

"What will?"

"The fuckin acid Frankie. The fuckin acid."

It's as hot as an inflamed arsehole, and I'm in some jazz club, but there are no people.

"Where are the people?" I ask, and nobody answers. Maybe they arrive when the music starts.

There's saxophone music playing loudly. Robson says that the sax player is world-class and one of the best sax players he's ever heard.

"Is this Bangkok, then?" I ask, but Robson is still going on about Mike's career as a jazz saxophonist.

"He's one of the best," Robson says. "Well known in the industry. I've been comin' 'ere to watch him for years."

"To Bangkok?" I say.

"There's no saxophone," Borat tells us.

He's right. It's just the air conditioner in the limo. That's unbelievable. He turns around to us, and now he does look like Michael Caine in Zulu, and it's terrifying. I start to panic.

"How can you be Michael Caine?" I say. "Does anybody have any water? I need water"

Robson hands me a bottle, and I gulp it down. I quickly realise it's absinthe, and I spit it into Michael Caine's face.

"Are you one of those fire-breathers?" Robson, The Giant Badger says, laughing.

"Do you mean a dragon or one of those circus people that spits flames or a gang member?" I ask.

Michael Caine is wiping his face upfront.

It feels like my head is filled with bees. They are buzzing hard and trying to get out. I open my mouth and try and push them out with my tongue, but they buzz harder.

"Robson, is there any way to stop a trip?" I ask, wondering how much deeper it's going to go.

The giant badger is just laughing.

I try to ask Caine but he's not there.

"Michael Caine?" I yell, "Michael Caine? Michael Caine? Michael Caine?"

I wonder why I am shouting Michael Caine, and now Robson The Badger starts shouting, "Michael Caine, Michael Caine, Michael Caine!"

I realise we are both yelling Michael Caine continuously, and none of us knows why, so I burst into laughter

The jazz is blaring, but the people still haven't arrived in Bangkok, so I close my eyes and listen to the waves of the saxophone go up and down, and I begin to see the notes and scales appear before my eyes with the music.

"John Coltrane," I shout. "John Coltrane, John Coltrane, John,"

Then I remember we are back in the limo again, and the music is just the air conditioner.

Robson is sitting up and trying to light a cigarette with the Absinthe bottle.

"We're in the back of the limo," I tell him. I realise I have his plastic lighter, and I reach out and light his cigarette for him. Then I close my eyes and lie down.

Robson is slapping my face, and my eyes creep open again.

"We're here," he says. I don't know what he means by that. I feel good, but I realise I disappeared for some time then in quite a deep way.

"Why aren't you in your tux?" I ask Robson. "Isn't there a dress code at these events?"

"There is, Mate, yeah," he says. "Mike, where is my tux?" But Mike still isn't there. Was Mike ever there? I look into the front at an empty seat and a cigarette still burning in the ashtray.

"There's only a cigarette," I yell. Maybe Mike *is* a cigarette.

Robson pushes himself between the two chairs next to me.

"What do we do?" I ask him.

It sounds like hail is coming down on the roof of the limo, and the thunder and lightning are getting bad out there.

"It's not nightclub weather," I say. "Is this Bangkok?"

The door opens suddenly, and Robson and I leap in terror. I see the flashing lights of the paparazzi, and I remember that I'm Robson's bodyguard. I need to muster some courage and keep him safe. I step forward into the flashing lights, but my foot goes down a grid, and I slam my face into the car door.

It's embarrassing, and I know I'm going to be in all the papers tomorrow. I can see it now,

Robson's bodyguard smashes his face at the Oscars.

That's my career over, I guess. Still, I feel good. I want to disappear again, but Saddam pulls me up. This must be Bangkok.

Robson is cowering in the corner of the Limo.

"Remember when you were young? I say to him, leaning back in. "Remember that cocky young fearless actor? That guy is still in there somewhere, right?"

"Yer fuckin reet Jimmy," Robson says in a Scottish accent, grabbing my hand and pulling himself out of the limo. He shuffles past me, and people start taking pictures as he stands there waiting for assistance. I put my arm around him and start pushing people away aggressively.

"What are you doing?" Saddam says. I remember I'm in Iraq covering the war, and I start bowing to Saddam.

"Excuse me, your Honour," I say. "I seem to have lost my camera,"

I bow again and again. I know I should be taking pictures, but I can't find my damn camera. I can hear the bombs dropping and the bullets flying overhead.

There are more people gathering around now, and they are trying to get to Robson. He is gripping a signpost tightly and has gone pale white with his eyes closed. I know I have to do my job regardless of the consequences, so I pull out my phone and call my secretary on speed dial.

"Hello, Frank,"

"Send assistance immediately. I'm stuck in Iraq, and Saddam is trying to torture Robson. There are bees trying to escape my head, and I keep disappearing. I am afraid I might *want* to die."

I feel the tears streaming down my cheeks. There is another bang, and I hit the deck, covering my head and dropping my phone. I try to grab it, but there are several phones on the ground.

"hello, hello," comes the voice. Oh, I still have my phone.

"I'm so sorry," I say. " I'm dying in Iraq. Things aren't looking good at all. I just want to say thank you for my life, and I love you."

I'm balling like a child.

"Frank, what the hell is happening?" she says.

"I have to go, Mum. I love you".

The moment I hang up the phone, I remember who I am. I'm Frank, and this is meant to be therapy. We are outside the night-club called 'Bangkok' for Robson's award ceremony. I laugh.

"We're not in Iraq," I scream at Robson. He has a badger head again, but the rest of his body is normal. Saddam is trying to peel Robson's arms off the signpost, and I know he is going to take him away and torture him. But I see the paparazzi lights start flashing again.

"It's okay, mate." I say to Robson. I want to tell him he is a brilliant director and he will probably win for his film, whatever it was called.

"Thanks, Jimmy Man. I love you," Robson says in his Scottish accent. I take one of his arms while Borat takes the other, and we smile and wave and walk up to the front door of the venue where the awards are happening.

Paparazzi and fans are trying to grab Robson, and I remember I'm his bodyguard, so I push them away again. I grab one of them by the shirt, but Borat tells me to stop. I trust him. He must have been to hundreds of these ceremonies.

We fall through the front door into what seems like pitch black, with severe algorithmic equations coming out of the darkness. We're standing at this counter, and these demonic eyes come out of the darkness. Robson falls back in fright and bangs his head on the wall behind him. I want to protect him, but I'm terrified. I remember that we died in the limo crash on the way to Bangkok, and we are entering hell.

I make a run for the entrance, but I crash into the glass door, and Saddam grabs the back of my jacket and pulls me in, screaming and begging for one more chance.

• • • • • • • • •

I can't say what happened in the last hour, but I know we are in an actual bar — probably Bangkok, and I am Frank.

The music is unbelievable, and I have forgotten what year it is. It feels like the future, but I can't be sure.

There's a silhouette of a cowboy dancing with a bullwhip on one wall, and I'm in the middle of this dance floor, soaked in euphoria. My Grandpa is shanking in every corner of this bar. I see him clearly when I close my eyes — endless shanking grandpas one inside another, everywhere.

I see *her* too. It's Dana. I can't believe it. I look harder and think it must be the trip, but its *definitely* her.

I push my way through the dance floor and sit down right next to her on this purple couch. I pull out a cigarette, and she lights it for me. I don't know what to say to her. I should probably say *thanks*.

"Crash and burn, Maverick," I say instead, and she smiles at me.

I don't know why I said that.

"What do you want?" she says.

I guess I can't blame her for being mad. I see the atoms of her body clearly, and at the centre of every atom is a shanking Grandpa.

She is a divine Goddess.

"I'm sorry for everything," I say.

"What are you talking about?" she says.

I'm trying to think about what I'm apologising for. I don't think I did anything wrong. We just had sex. Then I remember trying to look up her skirt, and I feel like an idiot.

"I'm sorry I tried to look up your skirt," I say. "But the red lace was *surprising*."

She takes a drag of her cigarette and leans over to her friend, who bends forward and checks me out.

"You're Ace's friend, aren't you?"

I wondered where the old badger head was.

"Actually, his name is Robson," I tell them, "and I'm his psychologist. He has herpes, you know?" I'm not laughing anymore. None of it seems funny.

Dana's friend leaves, and I lean in to kiss Dana on the lips, but she pushes me off. I feel someone grab the back of my shirt and pull me up. It's Mike.

"What the hell?" I say. "Let go of me. I found *Dana* in here."

I swing around and point to an empty seat.

"It's not fuckin Dana," Robson tells me. "You were all over some girl. People thought you were trying to assault her. You need to get a grip, Pal."

"I wasn't, I swear. It was *Dana*."

I follow Mike and Robson out to a private corner of the club. There are three or four or five other people out there, and a joint comes around, so I take a long drag and pass it on. Then, someone hands me a tiny bottle of something, and I take a big sniff.

"Take it fucking easy, Man," a young stranger says to me.

I don't even know what I just sniffed.

I thought I was straightening out, but *whatever that stuff is* — kicks in, and I'm tripping all over again, but it feels different. It's cleaner and slightly more gothically horny.

Robson leans into me. He has a new girl on each arm, and his luminous hair is flowing and glinting under the lights. I don't feel *right* calling him Robson anymore. This is his pure realm now. Look at him — he is *beautiful*. He is a god in this place, if only for a while, drugged up and surrounded by worshippers and lovers. I understand why they worship him. This is like a god realm.

I am suddenly gripped by the idea that this is going to end, and I will have to go back to work even though I'd rather stay here with this rock n roll god.

"You've gotta fuckin call her Pal," Ace says.

It feels like *God* is talking to me.

"Tell her how you feel. It doesn't matter if you lose her. If you do, it was *never* meant to be. You can't go having fuckin elephants in the room, Frankie. You gotta dress the cunts up and make them dance."

"I can't lose her," I tell him. "I *love* her."

"You don't fuckin love her, Pal. Your *cock* loves her, and she's got her fuckin fishhook right in your fuckin nuts. That wasn't *Dana* in there. She's just seeping into your consciousness."

He looks at me and nods.

"All of this, it ain't you, My Brother. This life, the booze, the stragglers. You're *beyond* all this." He reaches out his hand and takes hold of mine. I feel his energy surging through me. I feel so connected to him.

"Go *home,* Frank," he says. "Then *call* her. Tell her *everything* and set the record straight. You wanna know a secret?"

"What's that?"

"You ain't a fuckin therapist, Pal."

"I know. I told *you* that," I say.

"No, I mean it ain't your *calling* in life. "

"Oh yeah, well, what is?"

He lets go of my hand and leans back, putting his arms around each girl while I await his celestial insight.

"Don't fuckin know, Pal. But I know you need to go set the record straight."

I smile and stare at his beautiful face for a minute.

"You said the acid would sort my life out," I say.

"Nah, I didn't. I said it would put you back where you need to be,"

It's true. He did say that.

"This is your reality, Frankie. You have to accept it before you can release it, you know?"

I nod and smile, and I feel a glint of that most elusive sensation — happiness. And for a blissful eternity, our infinite friendship locks in.

He's *right* — I'm *not* the therapist. I'm the *patient*.

"Here," he says to the unfathomably beautiful redhead on his left. "Go give him a big fuckin kiss from me, would you?"

A copper-haired goddess in a dark green dress stands up, puts her arm around me and presses her lips against mine. Existence drops away, and it's just me and her rising into the sky. Her tongue feels like a million years of gentle, uncomplaining rainfall. Then, as she pulls away so softly, looking into my eyes for a moment, smiling and holding me like my mother, I weep like her child as I think of the people and the animals and the fact that we are all separate and how we can't be together indefinitely and how that is the worst thing in the world and how we all react to that trauma in different ways. And I think that, for the first time, I realise the purpose of therapy, and I promise myself that I will do whatever it takes to free them all of their pain.

I thank her without words.

"I'm fuckin doomed, Frankie," Ace shouts suddenly. "It's too late for me, Pal. But you can save yourself."

I nod at him, at each of the girls and at Michael Caine, who is standing there, uninterested and drinking a bottle of water.

Shanking Grandpa is long gone. He took the bliss with him, but the clarity remains. Standing here in this sweaty psychedelic club, I don't feel sorry for myself anymore. I've never been fundamental about rebirth or anything like that, but for a moment, I remember Ace from all of our past meetings and all of our future meetings, and I know it's time to leave.

"See you for next week's session," I say with a grin.

He pulls out a packet of Marlboros and hands me one. I light his and mine and give him his cheap plastic lighter back.

I head across the dance floor of wrecked citizens, drenched in their own bliss, soaked in their own misfortune, crushed by the weight of their own pathetic duality. On the other side of the floor, I reach the exit and put my shaking hand on the door handle and turn around one last time, hopefully. And, there he is, the King of Bliss with his two consorts, still watching me, still giving me *all* of his attention.

I *needed* that.

We nod one last time and I turn and walk up the dark corridor and open the door at the end. It's so bright. It feels strange that the sun is still up. I look at my watch. It's 2.46 pm, and I have a bunch of missed calls from Janice. I'm going to need a good reason for this.

"Find your way back out of Iraq, did you?" she says as she answers the phone.

· · · · · · · · · · ·

I've felt this feeling before, but not for a long time. I have swollen gums and a horrendous headache down one side of my head. Down the other side is numb, and it's buzzing like an angry wasp. I check my voicemail, and the first one is from Dana.

Hi Frank. Thanks for your message. I've been at a conference and just got in.

What message? This can't be good.

First, I appreciate your honesty.

No elephants in the room, right?

At the same time. You're a real cunt for putting me in that position.

Oh right. Well, at least there is a reaction. Maybe she *does* have feelings for me and —

Obviously, I can't put you forth for any role now, knowing you are a fraud.

Ho. I was *not* expecting that.

Even worse, I could lose my licence if I don't turn you in —

There is silence. Elephants.

— but look, I won't, okay? Still, it means I can't see you anymore. I had a good time with you, Frank. And look, I insist you get out there, do something different. You should get into recruiting.

You don't need to be qualified for that. Okay, delete this message asap, won't you? Alright, take care.

That's it.

And I just stand there for a minute, *feeling* it.

Would you believe it? Old Robson was *right.* No elephants.

I know that I can't do my job anymore. I didn't realise that. I thought I was *trapped*, but I'm not. I'm *free*.

He was right about Dana too. My cock was in love with her.

The acid took me to where I am supposed to be — right here in my apartment at 6.05 am today. Right now.

I don't want to drink. I don't need Dana. I don't need my job.

I just need to see what comes up for a while.

ACKNOWLEDGMENTS

Thanks to my friends who gave this a good read and slagged it before it got published: Mike 'The Kid' Knittel, Terry Day, Gemma Lee and her lovely mum, the psychedelic jazz legend Arthur Rosche and his boy Gabriel. Thanks to the celestial eyeballs of Ann James for understanding Frank and offering editing suggestions without financial reward. Thanks to the Young Birds for endless inspiration, The Guru DC, My precious parents and siblings, nephews and nieces, The Brown Shell, The Dark Pigeon, Mr Grumpy, The Norwegian Heart, The Witches of the West, The Russian Dragon, Bobby Flynn, The One From Burma, Kenny and the crew. To the awakened beings, gods, demigods, humans, animals, ghosts and tortured beings of this and the other worlds who inspired this and my other stories.

All I can say is thanks and — sorry.

FTB